# TEN LUCKY LEPRECHAUNS

by Kathryn Heling and
Deborah Hembrook

illustrated by Jay Johnson

**CARTWHEEL BOOKS**
an imprint of Scholastic Inc.

For Ben and Nora — because of you, I'm the luckiest grandma in the world!—KEH

To my niece, Lindsey Mae — you are a treasure to me and our family! — Love, DKH

For my parents, wife, Cristy, and my sons, Kyle & Nathan—JJ

Text copyright © 2012 by Kathryn Heling and Deborah Hembrook.
Illustrations copyright © 2012 by Scholastic Inc.

All rights reserved. Published by Scholastic Inc. SCHOLASTIC, CARTWHEEL BOOKS, and associated logos are trademarks and/or registered trademarks of Scholastic Inc.

ISBN 978-0-545-43648-9

28 27 26                    21

Printed in the U.S.A.    40
First printing, February 2012

The woods are full of leprechauns,
And treasures to uncover.
Fiddle-de-fizz, there's magic, there is,
When leprechauns find each other.

One leprechaun hears a noisy wee elf,
Who's playing a squawky kazoo.
Fiddle-de-fizz, 'tis magic, it is!

Two leprechauns find a busy wee elf,
Who's painting an orange spotted tree.
Fiddle-de-fizz, 'tis magic, it is!

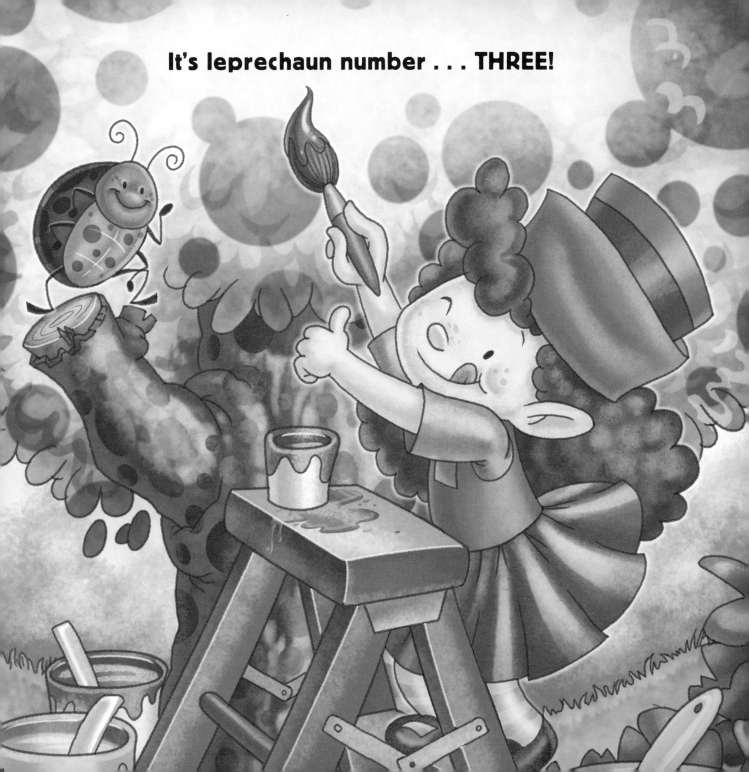

Three leprechauns spy a nimble wee elf,
Who romps on the green forest floor.
Fiddle-de-fizz, 'tis magic, it is!

It's leprechaun number . . . FOUR!

Four leprechauns see a silly wee elf,
Who splats in a belly-flop dive.
Fiddle-de-fizz, 'tis magic, it is!

It's leprechaun number . . . FIVE!

Five leprechauns watch a jolly wee elf,
Who's practicing juggling tricks.
Fiddle-de-fizz, 'tis magic, it is!

It's leprechaun number . . . SIX!

Six leprechauns spot a speedy wee elf,
Who zooms by – engines a revvin'!
Fiddle-de-fizz, 'tis magic, it is!

It's leprechaun number . . . SEVEN!

Seven leprechauns glimpse a lively wee elf,
Who's balancing on the old gate.
Fiddle-de-fizz, 'tis magic, it is!

It's leprechaun number . . . EIGHT!

Eight leprechauns view a frisky wee elf,
Who's zipping through trees on a vine.
Fiddle-de-fizz, 'tis magic, it is!

It's leprechaun number . . . NINE!

Nine leprechauns meet a clever wee elf,
Who's hunting for treasure and then,
Fiddle-de-fizz, 'tis magic, it is!

**It's leprechaun number . . . TEN!**

Ten leprechauns find a big pot of gold
At the place where the bright rainbow ends.
But fiddle-de-fizz, the true magic is . . .

**Finding ten lucky leprechaun friends!**